A Story about
Color Blindness

by Julie Anderson

illustrated by
David López

Albert Whitman & Company
Chicago, Illinois

For James and Erik, of course.—J.A.

To Lulan, the most
shiny and colorful nephew.—D.L.

Erik the Red was a wonderful kid. Ask anyone.

He wondered if fish got thirsty. He wondered why he couldn't tickle himself. He wondered if he could make his friend Miles start hiccupping from laughter again today. Sometimes he wondered what life would be like without a nickname, but from the day he was born he was Erik the Red.

Lately he wondered why everything seemed to be going wrong. "Erik the Red, kick to your team instead!" yelled Coach when Erik passed the ball to the other team.

"Erik the Red, is your brain still in bed?" Ms. Dalton asked when he handed in the wrong reading homework or skipped half the math problems.

"I thought I was paying attention," said Erik. "Why do I keep getting things wrong?"

"Everyone makes mistakes," said his mom. "Maybe you could write down the assignments better."

He wondered if there was anything else he could possibly muddle. Unfortunately, there was: a pop quiz in math.

"Erik the Red, keep your eyes ahead," his friend Annabel whispered.

Mom was called to school. Erik explained he wasn't looking at the answers, just the problems Annabel copied because he couldn't read them from the board.

"You could see the board last year, right?" his mom asked.

"Maybe I was sitting closer," Erik said, "I could see everything on the nurse's eye chart, but I can't see Ms. Dalton's writing sometimes. I wonder why."

"So do I," said his mother.

There was one class that made him happy—art class.
There nobody said, "You're such a silly blockhead, Erik the Red!"

Until…

"Is that you?" His friend Sam pointed and asked. "You are supposed to draw you, not a monster instead!"

"That's very imaginative," the art teacher said. "Sometime I wonder what goes on in your head, Erik the . . .

"…Green?!"

"That's just about the funniest thing I've ever seen, Erik the…Green!"

"What do you mean?" asked Erik. "That's the color it's always been."

Everyone was laughing. Except for Erik. And somebody else, too.

"Erik," said Annabel, "you're color-blind, aren't you?"

"I see colors," Erik replied. "I'm not blind."

"It's okay, my dad is color-blind, too." Annabel smiled. "I get to pick out his socks and ties."

When Erik brought his portrait home that night he told his mom and dad what Annabel said.

His parents looked at the picture, then looked at each other.

They went to the computer.

They went to the doctor.

Then Erik and his parents went back to his teachers.

Erik had been paying attention in school, his mom and dad told the teachers, but many shades of brown, green, gold, and orange—like the color of Erik's red hair—looked very similar to Erik. Color-coding makes school easier for most kids, but not Erik.

Erik's room

What Erik sees

Pencils and pens at school

How Erik sees them

Even food can look different!

"So do you only see in black and white?" asked Miles.

"I see colors," Erik explained to the class. "I just see them differently than most people. The eye doctor said that what I have used to be called color blindness but is called color vision deficiency or color vision confusion these days. I like to think I am color vision quirky!

"I have always heard people talk about colors, like gold or olive, and never understood how they agreed which was which," Erik explained. "If I put them right next to each other, I could see they were a little different, but I was amazed at how fast other people could tell them apart without studying them."

"Can the doctor change your eyes to see like other kids?"

"No, but there are other ways to help me."

Erik's mom and dad looked through his schoolbooks. In his math book some problems were printed in red ink on a green background. Erik didn't see them!

Ms. Dalton made black-and-white copies of those pages. Now Erik had no problem seeing all the problems.

The reading assignments were on color-coded file cards in color-coded boxes. Erik couldn't tell them apart.

The class wrote out the names of the colors on all the cards and boxes. Now Erik didn't have to wonder if he was doing the correct reading assignment.

Last year the chalkboard in his classroom was black—this year it was green. When the teacher wrote with yellow chalk, Erik couldn't read what was on the board.

"I'm sorry," said Ms. Dalton. "You told me the truth, and I didn't understand."

"That's okay." Erik smiled. "I didn't understand either. White chalk makes it no problem at all!"

The green and orange practice vests Erik had a hard time telling apart in the heat of a game…

…were replaced with blue and white instead. Erik never passed to the wrong side again…at least not on purpose.

"Do you want me to write the color names on all the paints?" Annabel asked Erik in art class.

"That would be nice, thank you. But you know, mostly I like to use colors as I see them, not as other people do."

"Then that's what you should do, Erik the…Erik the…"

"BLUE!" they laughed together.
"Just Erik is fine," said Erik.

All about color and vision

How do we see color?

In the back of your eye, in a part called the retina, are tiny cells called rods and cones. Rods and cones take in everything you see and turn it into information that is sent to your brain. The cones allow you to recognize color.

There are three kinds of cones—green, red, and blue. The cones mix colors, working together to help you see countless different shades. If one or more of the kinds of cones are missing or aren't working properly, your brain receives different information than most people. You have color vision deficiency (CVD).

Who has color vision deficiency?

For every one girl who is color-blind, there are about twenty boys who are. About one out of twelve boys has some degree of CVD.

Why do more boys have color vision deficiency?

Ninety-nine percent of cases are red-green deficiencies, like Erik has. This type is inherited from parents—like curly hair or blue eyes. It is present from birth and is permanent.

Boys are affected more because the X chromosome carries CVD. Girls have two X chromosomes—boys have one X and one Y chromosome. Chromosomes include all the information from your parents that make you, you. If a boy's one X chromosome includes color defective information he will be color deficient, but a girl must inherit two color defective X chromosomes to be color deficient. The other one percent of CVD cases includes very rare blue deficiencies and even rarer true color blindness—when a person sees only shades of black, white, and gray. These affect both boys and girls with the same frequency.

Do all people with red-green color vision deficiency see the same?

No! CVD is categorized as slight, moderate, severe, or absolute. Erik would most likely be categorized as moderate to severe. People with slight CVD can go for years without realizing it unless they are tested.

How is color vision tested?

An optometrist or an ophthalmologist does a full eye exam to diagnose CVD. The most well known test for red-green color deficiency was developed by Dr. Shinobu Ishihara in 1917. Ishihara tests have different colored dots arranged in a pattern that displays a number—a number that may not be visible to a person with CVD. The test can even be used on young children who do not know numbers yet but can trace the pattern with their fingers.

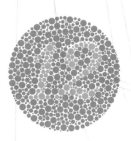 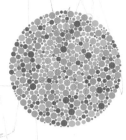

Most people can see the numeral 12 in this image.

But people with some kinds of CVD will not be able to see it in this image.

Can color vision deficiency be cured?

Scientists are working on it, but there is no cure for CVD at this time. Color correcting lenses and glasses to reduce glare help some people distinguish shades, but they don't enable the wearer to see the colors as other people without CVD do.

How can I help a person with CVD?

People with CVD learn how to interpret the world they see, even if it is different from what you see. If they ask you if something matches, tell them! But try to resist the urge to quiz them—"What color is my shirt?" or "What color is that car?"—because you are curious. People with CVD agree that gets old fast!

Library of Congress Cataloging-in-Publication Data

Anderson, Julie.
Erik the red sees green / by Julie Anderson ; illustrated by David Lopez.
pages cm
Summary: When Erik begins having problems in school and on the soccer field, he discovers that he is color blind.
[1. Color blindness—Fiction. 2. School–Fiction.] I. Lopez, David, illustrator. II. Title.
PZ7.A5393Eri 2013 [E]—dc23 2013005187

Text copyright ©2013 by Julie Anderson.
Illustrations copyright ©2013 by Albert Whitman & Company.
Published in 2013 by Albert Whitman & Company.
ISBN 978-0-8075-2141-0

Printed in China.

10 9 8 7 6 5 4 3 2 1 NP 18 17 16 15 14 13

For more information about Albert Whitman & Company,
visit our web site at www.albertwhitman.com.